Hi! I'm Darcy J. Doyle, Daring Detective,

but you can call me D.J. The only thing I like better than reading a good mystery is solving one. When my brother, Allen, got blamed for turning over garbage cans and putting eggs in mailboxes, I had to do something about it. Let me tell you about The Case of the Mixed-Up Monsters.

Other books in the Darcy J. Doyle, Daring Detective series:

Darcy J. Doyle
Daring Detective

The Case of the
Mixed-Up Monsters

Linda Lee Maifair

ZondervanPublishingHouse
Grand Rapids, Michigan

A Division of HarperCollins*Publishers*

Requests for information should be addressed to:
Zondervan Publishing House
Grand Rapids, Michigan 49530

Library of Congress Cataloging-in-Publication Data

Maifair, Linda Lee.
    The case of the mixed-up monsters / Linda Lee Maifair.
        p. cm. — (Darcy J. Doyle, Daring Detective)
    Summary: When neighbors claim to have seen her brother
Allen, dressed in his Halloween monster costume, committing
acts of vandalism, Darcy Doyle vows to find out who's framing
him.
    ISBN 0-310-57921-X
    [1. Halloween—Fiction. 2. Mystery and detective stories.]
I. Title. II. Series: Maifair, Linda Lee. Darcy J. Doyle, Daring
Detective.
PZ7.M2776Cau   1993
[Fic]—dc20   92-39013
                                                    CIP
                                                    AC

Edited by Lori J. Walburg
Interior design by Rachel Hostetter
Illustrations by Tim Davis

Printed in the United States of America

93 94 95 96 97 / ❖ LP / 10 9 8 7 6 5 4 3 2 1

With love, for my son,
George Richard,
my life's greatest miracle and blessing.
Like Darcy's faithful bloodhound, Max,
he's fun to be with
and always ready to help
with my next big project.
I'm proud of him.

CHAPTER 1

I'm Darcy J. Doyle. Some of my friends call me Darcy. Some just call me D.J. If I keep solving important cases, pretty soon everyone will be calling me Darcy J. Doyle, Daring Detective. It's only a matter of time.

My last big case started when I was trying on my costume for the Bayside Halloween party. Dad's old trench coat. Mom's old riding cap. Grandpa's pipe.

"How do I look?" I asked my faithful bloodhound, Max. I held up a half-eaten chocolate chip cookie, left over from lunch.

Max woofed his approval. Good old Max. I threw him the cookie just as my brother, Allen, stomped into my room.

"It's not fair!" Allen said, then wrinkled up his nose when he saw me. "What are *you* supposed to be?"

I thought it was obvious. "Sherlock Holmes," I told him.

Allen laughed. Hard. "You look more like—"

I gave him one of my looks. He didn't finish. He plopped belly-down on my bed. "It isn't fair!" he said again.

Ordinarily I would have chased him out of the room, but my Daring Detective mind was curious. "What's not fair?" I asked him. "And get your smelly sneakers off my pillow!"

He didn't even argue that his sneakers weren't smelly. "Mrs. Carson told Dad I turned over her garbage cans last night. Now Dad says maybe I shouldn't go to the Halloween party."

I knew how much he wanted to go. He had a good chance of winning the Best Costume prize the second year in a row. Even I had to admit that his Alien Monster costume was terrific.

"So why did you knock over the cans?" I asked him.

"I didn't!" he said. He even sounded as if he meant it.

"Are you sure?" I asked anyway. It was the sort of thing Allen might do.

He stood up, looking insulted. "Of course I'm sure!"

"Then why would Mrs. Carson say you did?"

"She says she saw me, Darcy. With her own eyes. But she couldn't have, because I wasn't there! I was doing my homework."

I knew he must be telling the truth. Even Allen wouldn't be dumb enough to make up a story about homework. Nobody would believe an alibi like that.

I smiled. If Allen didn't knock over the cans, somebody else must have. It was beginning to sound like a perfect case for Darcy J. Doyle, Daring Detective.

"If I miss the party, I won't win first prize!" Allen said. "And it's ten whole dollars!"

"Hmmm." Ten whole dollars, and he could give some of it to me. I put a hand on his shoulder. "You've come to the right place, Allen," I told him. Ordinarily I never call him Allen, but a detective can't call a client "Pest"—even if he is one.

"I have?" he said.

"Sure," I told him. "You've been framed. And I'm going to unframe you."

"You are?" he said.

I nodded. "My faithful bloodhound, Max, and I will find the real culprit." I smiled again. "And it will only cost you two dollars."

He didn't exactly jump at the offer. "Two dollars!"

"If you would rather miss the Halloween party . . ." I shrugged as if it really didn't matter to me . . . as if I didn't need the two dollars to buy the new mystery book I wanted.

"Well . . ."

I could tell he was weakening. "I'm even giving you a special rate, since you're my brother," I said. Not bothering to tell him that my usual rate was a dollar, I took off my costume and motioned him toward the door.

"I guess it *might* be worth two dollars to—"

I didn't give him time to change his mind. "Come on," I said, using my best Daring Detective voice. "We have just enough time to interrogate the witness before dinner."

"To do what to who?"

I picked up my detective's notebook and pencil. "We're going to talk to Mrs. Carson."

Max was already whining and scratching at the front door when we got there. Good old Max. Always anxious to help Darcy J. Doyle, Daring Detective, tackle her next big case.

CHAPTER 2

Mrs. Carson gave me one of those looks adults give you when they think you're being "cute."

"Daring Detective?" she said. "How cute."

"Allen's been framed," I told her. "I'm going to prove he's innocent."

She shook her head. "Oh, I'm afraid not, dear," she said. She scowled at Allen. "I saw him with my own eyes. Just like I told your father. Throwing garbage all over the place. Making all kinds of noise. I'd recognize that costume anywhere."

"Hmmm," I said. I took out my notebook and pencil. "Can you describe it for me?"

Mrs. Carson frowned as if I weren't being cute anymore. "I've got dinner on the stove, and—"

"Please?" I said. "It won't take long."

She sighed. "Everyone knows what his costume looks like, Darcy! He's shown it off all over the neighborhood. It's rusty brown and all furry."

Mrs. Carson pointed a finger at Max, sniffling around near her garbage can. Good old Max. Always looking for clues. "Like your dog," Mrs. Carson said.

"Hmmm." Allen's costume *was* rusty brown and furry, like Max. He'd made it out of an old moth-eaten coat my mother found in the attic. I started to write *circumstantial evidence* in my notebook, but I couldn't spell it. I didn't ask Mrs. Carson how, either.

"Hmmm," I said instead. "Did anyone else see it?"

Mrs. Carson scowled at me this time. "*I* saw it, young lady. That should be enough. If you don't believe *me* you can ask Willie. He saw it, too."

Mrs. Carson waggled a finger under Allen's nose. "Your father told me it wouldn't happen again. It better not, young man! What a mess! Lucky for you my Willie helped me clean it up. You don't find *him* going around the neighborhood causing trouble."

She closed the door without even saying good-bye.

"Willie's a pain," Allen muttered under his breath.

My Sunday school teacher, Mrs. Benson, says there's good in everybody if we look hard enough. But for once, I had to agree with Allen. Willie Carson was a pain.

"He's also a witness," I said. "We'll have to interrogate him, too."

I looked around for Max. He had the lid off Mrs. Carson's garbage can. His whole head was inside. "Good old Max," I told him, taking him by the collar, dragging him away. "Always on the job."

CHAPTER 3

We found Willie in the garden shed. We could hear his radio, but we couldn't see him. He had a picture of a skull taped over the window. Under the skull were the words KEEP OUT OR ELSE. We pounded on the door until Willie came out.

"Go away," he said. "I'm working on my costume and I don't want nobody stealing my idea." He smiled a mean sort of smile at Allen. "I'm not coming in second this year."

Max tried to push his way into the shed. Willie sneezed three times. "Get that mutt out of here," he said. "I'm allergic." He sneezed again, twice, as if to prove it.

I shoved Max toward our backyard. "Go home, Max," I told him. He trotted off in the opposite direction. Probably looking for more clues. I could use some. Good old Max.

"You're going to be more than allergic if you keep talking to my faithful bloodhound, Max, like that," I warned Willie. "He's a trained attack animal, you know."

Willie laughed. "He wouldn't attack a flea." He wiped his nose on the back of his sleeve. "And he's no bloodhound, he's just an old—"

I gave him one of my looks. He didn't finish.

"Your mom says you saw the culprit who turned over the garbage cans last night."

Willie smiled his mean smile again. "Yeah. Plain as day. I was working here in the shed and heard the noise. Looked out the window and saw *him* in that dumb costume of his. Turning over the cans. Dumping out the garbage. I didn't want to tell Mom." He grinned. "But what else could I do?"

"It wasn't me, Willie Carson!" Allen held a fist under Willie's nose.

I almost wished he'd bop him, but he was in enough trouble already. "Allen . . ." I warned him.

"He just made it up," Allen said, looking as if he was going to clobber Willie after all.

Willie thought so too. He backed toward the shed door. "I . . . I didn't make it up. Mom saw you, too. I gotta go finish my costume." He ran into the shed and slammed the door behind him.

"It wasn't me, Darcy," Allen told me. He looked pretty desperate.

I felt pretty desperate myself. At this rate I'd never solve the case . . . or get my two dollars.

"I believe you," I said. We Daring Detectives always say things like that, even when our

clients look really guilty. And we never give up till the case is solved. This one could take a long time, and we only had three days till Halloween. "I—"

CRASH! BANG! CLATTER!

Allen and I ran in the direction of the loud, metallic noises coming from Mrs. Carson's back porch. We got there just in time to see Mrs. Carson chasing Max out of the yard with a broom. The garbage cans were knocked over again, and torn-up garbage was everywhere.

I groaned. It hadn't taken nearly as long as I thought. "I think I've solved The Case of the Clattering Cans," I told Allen.

He wasn't impressed. It was so obvious he figured it out himself. "I'm not paying you two dollars when it was your dog who—"

He didn't get to finish.

"ALLEN RYAN DOYLE! GET OVER HERE THIS INSTANT!"

25

CHAPTER 4

It was never a good sign when Dad used your whole name. And I knew he was plenty mad to be yelling outside where everybody could hear him.

"What'd you do now?" I asked Allen. He didn't get to answer.

"ALLEN RYAN DOYLE, YOU HAVE FIVE SECONDS TO GET YOURSELF HOME!"

We made it over the hedge and across the yard in four seconds flat.

Dad pointed a finger at Allen's nose. "No Halloween party!"

"But—" Allen looked as if he were going to cry.

"Mrs. Robinson on Elm Avenue called a while ago. Said she saw you ringing doorbells there last night."

"But—" Allen didn't get any farther than he had the first time.

"And Bob Warren just left," Dad interrupted again, even though he always tells us it's not polite. "I guess you know what he came to see me about."

Allen didn't look as if he did. "No, I—"

Dad did it again. "Eggs! Eggs in the mailboxes. Every mailbox on Maple Avenue!" He shook his head at Allen as if he couldn't believe anybody could be that dumb, even Allen.

"But I didn't—" Allen tried again.

"Don't lie to me, Allen. I've had quite enough of your stories already."

I didn't think this was the time to point out

that Dad had interrupted four times in a row, though I did sort of wonder if he'd send himself to bed without dessert.

"I thought the garbage cans might be a mistake," Dad told Allen. "But this is too much. I told Mr. Warren you'll be over first thing in the morning to wash out his mailbox. *All* the mailboxes."

"But . . . it's Saturday!" Allen protested. "I'm going to play baseball with Tony and—"

"Oh no, you're not!" Dad was making a habit of interrupting. "The only place you're going for a while is to church and to school . . . and to Maple Avenue to wash eggs out of mailboxes. You're grounded for a week, young man." Dad went stomping back into the house.

"What am I going to do, Darcy?" Allen asked. "I didn't put eggs in anybody's mailbox. Not this year, anyway."

"Well," I said, trying to give my brightest,

most confident Daring Detective smile, "at least we know it wasn't Max."

"How do you know that?" he asked.

"Dogs don't put eggs in mailboxes or ring doorbells," I said. I frowned at my notebook. I didn't have a single clue. "You know, this case has gotten a whole lot more complicated. I don't know if two dollars is enough—"

Interrupting must be catching, like the flu. "You haven't even earned the two dollars yet!" Allen said. "All you've done so far is unframe a *dog!*" He stomped off toward the house, just like Dad had done.

I bent down and scratched Max behind the ear. "I'm sorry for thinking it was you," I told him. "Do you forgive me, boy?"

He licked my nose. Good old Max.

CHAPTER 5

I never knew old raw eggs could look so disgusting and smell so gross. I was sorry I had had scrambled eggs for breakfast.

"Thanks for helping, Darcy," Allen told me. He scraped dried eggshell off the inside of Mr. Warren's mailbox. It was hard work. The egg stuck like glue.

"Don't worry about it," I said. I figured it was the least I could do. I wasn't any closer to solving his case than I was before.

Mr. Warren came out to see how it was going. He bent over and peered into his damp mailbox. "Hmmm," he said.

That reminded me. I dropped my sponge into my bucket of soapy water, wiped my hand on my shirt, and pulled out my notebook.

"Do you have time to answer a few questions from Darcy J. Doyle, Daring Detective?" I asked Mr. Warren.

He looked at me as if I were a piece of dried hard egg yolk. "Daring what?" he asked.

"Detective," I said. "You know, like Sherlock Holmes? I'm trying to find out who framed Allen, and—"

"Nobody framed your brother," Mr. Warren said. "I saw him myself. Dressed in that monster costume of his." He shook his head at Allen. "With all that noise you were making . . . it was almost as if you wanted to be caught!"

It was my turn to say "Hmmm." I made a note in my notebook. Right next to *Brown and furry* and *Willie saw from shed. Wanted Allen caught,* I wrote. I frowned. It wasn't much to go on, even for a Daring Detective like me.

"You missed a spot." Mr. Warren pointed to a tiny bit of eggshell stuck to the top of the mailbox. He grinned and went back into his house.

Allen went back to his scraping. He did not look happy.

"What we need to do," I told him, "is catch the culprit in the act."

"Catch the who doing what?" he said.

"We've got to set a trap. Catch him red-handed."

"How do you plan to do that?" he asked.

I had no idea, but a Daring Detective doesn't admit things like that to a client. "Go to your room right after dinner," I told him. "I'll explain it then."

"I *have* to go to my room," he reminded me. "I'm grounded, remember?"

I started lugging the bucket to the next house

on Maple Avenue. I sighed. A half-dozen mail-boxes to go.

"Don't worry about a thing," I told Allen. "Darcy J. Doyle, Daring Detective, will take care of everything."

Allen made a face at me. *"That's* what I'm worried about!"

I stuffed the soggy sponge down the back of his shirt.

CHAPTER 6

Max and I tiptoed into Allen's room. "Put on some dark clothes," I told him. I was wearing a navy blue sweatshirt and jeans myself. "And help me take this blanket off your bed."

"Why?" he asked. We rolled the heavy dark wool blanket into a ball.

"Because that's what Daring Detectives always wear when they're out to catch a crook in the dark. And we'll need the blanket to throw over his head."

"Oh," Allen said, as if it made perfect sense to him. He covered his white T-shirt with a dark green jacket. "This okay?"

I nodded. "Come on."

The whole downstairs smelled like fresh-popped popcorn. Like any good bloodhound, Max noticed right away. He ran right by us, heading straight for the living room, where Mom and Dad were watching television. "Good old Max," I whispered to Allen. "He's creating a diversion."

"A what?" Allen whispered back.

"He's keeping Mom and Dad busy while we go catch the crook."

"I think he just wants some popcorn," Allen said.

I gave him one of my looks and shoved him out the door.

We spent the next half hour hiding behind bushes, arguing over whose turn it was to carry the blanket.

"What are we looking for anyway?" Allen asked me.

"Somebody acting suspicious," I told him.

"Don't you think we're acting sort of suspicious, Darcy? Hiding behind bushes, peeping into people's yards?"

If had a light I would have made a note in my notebook. *New Family Rate—three dollars.*

"We're allowed to act suspicious," I told him. "We're the good guys." I ran out from behind the bush and took a shortcut through the Carsons' backyard.

Allen followed, dragging the blanket behind him. The Carsons' porch light came on and we made a dive for the nearest bush. We watched as Willie, flashlight in hand, crossed the yard and went into the shed.

"He's sure spending a lot of time on that costume of his," I told Allen. "Maybe he'll win first prize this year."

"Sure he will!" Allen said. "Because I won't

be there. And neither will you if Dad finds us out here."

He had a point. "Let's make one more round of the neighborhood," I told him. "Dad's program will be over soon."

Allen complained the whole way. "What a waste of time. I'm cold. This won't do any good. And—"

CLATTER! BANG! CRASH!

We were nearly back home when we heard the commotion coming from the Carsons' driveway. We took off at a run, the blanket flapping between us. Panting, we hid behind one of the hedges again.

Mrs. Carson was standing on her porch, broom in hand, muttering at her overturned garbage can. Something big and furry ran by us.

"Get him!" I yelled to Allen.

"Which way did he go?" Allen yelled back.

I didn't know. "Listen! Over there! Don't let him get away."

We ran full speed around the corner of our house and knocked over somebody coming in the opposite direction. "Grab him!" I told Allen. "Throw the blanket over his head!"

We did, though it was a struggle. The culprit was a lot bigger and stronger than I expected.

"DARCY JESSAMYN DOYLE!" the culprit said, loudly.

I didn't really want to pull off the blanket, but I knew I had to. "Uh . . . Dad," I said, squinting at him in the darkness. "What are *you* doing here?"

He did not look amused. He took my shirt collar in one hand and Allen's jacket collar in the other and helped us to our back door.

Willie was waiting for us. "I saw the whole thing, Mr. Doyle," he said. He grinned, first at me, then at Allen. "They turned over the garbage. Both of them."

"I'll take care of it, William," Dad said. He sounded as if he planned to do just that.

CHAPTER 7

"I'll bet Sherlock Holmes never got grounded," I whispered to Allen as I passed him the collection plate.

Dad heard me. "I'll bet Sherlock Holmes never snuck out after dark," he said, even though we were in church and he wasn't supposed to be talking. "Or tackled his father."

"But—"

Dad gave me one of his looks. I turned to Mom for support, but she just stared me down, too. I decided it might be a real good idea to pay closer attention to Pastor Jordan's sermon.

On the way home we saw Mrs. Robinson raking leaves in her front yard. Dad pulled over to say hello.

"I hope your cold's better," she told Allen. "Such sneezing. Though it's no wonder, running around in the damp night air ringing doorbells."

Dad made Allen apologize.

Mrs. Robinson was real nice about it. "Boys will be boys," she said. "Why, I can remember when your father was a boy."

"We really have to go. Have a nice day," Dad said before Mrs. Robinson could finish telling us about the trouble he used to get into.

I was trying to imagine Dad ringing doorbells and putting eggs in mailboxes—and getting grounded—when Allen leaned over and whispered, "I don't have a cold, Darcy. I didn't have one two nights ago either." He looked at me as if that should mean something.

"So?"

"So maybe that's a clue," he said.

I hated to admit he was right. "Hmmm," I said instead.

"If we weren't grounded we could go around the neighborhood and see who has a cold," Allen suggested.

"Hmmm." I took out my notebook and read through my skimpy list of clues. *Brown and furry. Willie saw from shed. Wanted Allen caught.* I added *Culprit has a cold* and read the list twice before it made any sense.

I smiled. "Meet me in my room as soon as you change your clothes," I whispered to Allen. "And bring two dollars. Darcy J. Doyle, Daring Detective, has solved another case."

"You come to my room," Allen whispered back. "I'm grounded. For *two* weeks, thanks to Darcy J. Doyle, Daring Detective."

I was grounded for a week myself, but I

didn't want to argue the point. I needed the two dollars.

But when I came to his room, Allen refused to pay. "You don't get paid for figuring out who it is," he said stubbornly. "You only get paid if you prove it."

I made a note in my notebook. *Family Rate: three dollars. Pests two dollars extra.* "I'll prove it," I told Allen.

"How?" he wanted to know.

I had no idea. "You'll see," I told him. I gave him my most mysterious Daring Detective smile and sneaked back to my room.

CHAPTER 8

I could tell Willie was surprised by my phone call.

"What do you want?" he asked suspiciously.

"To see if you want to walk with me and Allen to the Halloween party tomorrow night," I told him.

"But . . . Mom said you were grounded. Both of you. She said your father told her—"

"Well, yeah, we are," I admitted. "Except for the party, you know. Dad said Allen worked so hard on his costume that he could go to the party after all . . . as long as nothing else happens."

"What do you mean?" Willie asked. He sounded real interested.

"As long as Allen doesn't get in any more trouble with the neighbors, he can still go," I explained.

"And if he gets in trouble?" Willie asked. He sounded as if he were looking forward to it.

"I guess somebody else will win first prize this year. But you don't have to worry about Allen. He's staying in his room all night just to be safe."

Willie didn't say anything.

"You want to walk with us or not?" I asked him.

"Uh, sure." He hung up without saying thanks or good-bye.

As soon as it was dark, Allen and I were out hiding behind the hedges again. Dad was working in his shop downstairs, and we'd sneaked by Mom while she was talking on the phone in the kitchen.

This time we brought Max with us. I figured

we might need him. He was whining and tug-ging at his leash, pulling in the direction of the Carson's driveway. Good old Max. Always so anxious to crack a really big case.

"What if Dad finds out?" Allen asked for the third time.

"Trust me," I said. "If we solve the case, you're off the hook."

"But what if we *don't?*" he whined. "I'll be grounded for the rest of my life!"

It wasn't being grounded that bothered me. I could see Dad and Mom's faces if they found out we'd sneaked out again.

"Do you really think we should—" Allen started again.

I didn't want to talk about it anymore. "Be quiet," I told him. "You're going to scare off our culprit."

Allen was quiet for all of five minutes.

"Look!" Allen said. He poked me in the ribs.

If he weren't a client who owed me two dollars, I might have poked him back. "I see him," I said.

Willie was walking toward the shed. For the first time in days, the moonlight was bright enough that he didn't need his flashlight. He looked in both directions, then slipped inside.

"What if he doesn't come out?" Allen whispered.

"He will," I said. After fifteen minutes I wasn't so sure.

Finally the shed door opened, slowly. A brown, furry form with two heads and four bobbing green antenna eyes crept out the door and started tiptoeing across the backyard, sneezing into his furry paw every few steps along the way.

"Get him!" I told Allen.

The monster whirled around in surprise, sneezed again, and took off across the yard.

"Fetch, Max!" I hollered, releasing the clasp on his leash.

Max ran off in the opposite direction. "Get him, Allen!"

Allen took off after Max. "Not the dog, dummy! The villain!" I jumped over the hedge and chased the monster myself, with Allen running a pace or two behind.

I caught up to him first, hiding behind a bush, trying to take off the costume between sneezes. I grabbed him, but he wriggled away. Allen tackled him from behind and sat on top of him.

I reached down and yanked off the furry brown two-headed mask.

CHAPTER 9

"I'll tell my mom!" Willie whined.

"Tell her what?" I asked. "That you turned over the garbage cans? And rang the doorbells? And put eggs in the mailboxes?"

"Why would I do that?" Willie asked.

Allen waved his fist under Willie's nose. "So you could blame it on me. So I'd miss the Halloween contest and you'd win first prize."

"I—I didn't . . ." Willie tried to squirm out from under Allen. He looked at me for help. I didn't feel like giving him any. "You got no proof," he said.

"We caught you wearing this." I held out the costume. "It's not as good as Allen's, but it looks a lot like it in the dark."

"I never—"

I didn't let him finish. "Mrs. Robinson said the doorbell ringer had a cold. Allen doesn't."

"Neither do I," Willie said.

"No," I agreed, sticking the costume under his nose. He sneezed three times before I could go on. "But you're allergic to fur," I said.

"It's your word against mine," Willie said. "Nobody will believe you."

"I will," a voice said.

"Uh . . . Dad, what are you doing here?" I asked for the second time. This time I was really sort of glad to see him.

"Max was scratching to get in. Ran right up the stairs and hid under your bed. When I saw that two kids who were grounded weren't in their rooms, I decided to bring Max out and investigate." He looked around the yard and shook his head. "I don't know where that dog went now."

Mrs. Carson came running across the yard with her broom. She stared down at my brother still sitting on Willie, pinning him to the ground. "You let Willie up, young man!" she said.

Since Mrs. Carson looked as if she might whap him with the broom, Allen did what she said. "What's going on here, John?" she asked my father. Dad explained.

"It wasn't me, Mom," Willie whined. "I told you, I was working on my costume, here in the shed."

"You also said you saw Allen from the window," I told him. "You've got a picture taped over the window so nobody can see in, Willie Carson. You can't see out either. It was all a lie."

Mrs. Carson grabbed Willie by the arm. "I'm

sorry, John," she told my father. "This won't happen again."

She dragged Willie toward the house. "Eggs in mailboxes!" she muttered. "Doorbells and garbage cans!"

"But, Mom . . . I really didn't knock over any garbage cans."

She didn't seem to believe him. She pushed him up the stairs and into the house, banging the door shut behind them.

Dad looked me in the eye. "You know you shouldn't have disobeyed me," he said.

Daring Detectives don't make many mistakes, but when we do, we aren't afraid to admit it. "I know, Dad. And I should have told you about Willie, too."

Dad's smile surprised me. "Yes, you should have. And I should have helped you catch the real culprit instead of blaming Allen for something he didn't do."

He put a hand on Allen's should. "I'm sorry I didn't listen to you, Son."

I gave Allen a poke, the way he'd done earlier to me. "Allen and I are sorry, too, Dad," I said. "Aren't we?" I asked Allen. Allen nodded.

"Shall we call it even?" Dad asked. We shook hands all around.

"I'll race you to the house," Dad said. "I think we might be able to talk Mom into giving us some ice cream before prayers.

Dad and Allen took off together at a run toward the hedge. Dad was leading all the way.

I didn't follow right away. I had to find Max first. It wasn't too hard.

CLATTER. CRASH. BANG.

I followed the noise to the Carson's driveway.

I straightened up the cans and picked up the garbage.

"Come on, Max," I said. "I'll race you home for ice cream."

I never had a chance. Max was over the hedge long before I got there. I smiled. Good old Max.

The next morning I asked Mrs. Carson to start putting something heavy on the lids of her trash cans.

That night Allen won second prize in the Halloween costume contest. Willie didn't go to the party. He was grounded for a whole month.

After the party, Allen paid me the two dollars. I only took one. After all, he only won five dollars, and he *is* my brother.

After a lot of coaxing, Dad even told us some of the things *he* used to do on Halloween.

But I never told anyone who the real clattering-cans culprit was. I just wrote it in my notebook, under Important Cases Solved by Darcy J. Doyle, Daring Detective.